Easter Egg Hunt

By Molly Kempf
Illustrated by MJ Illustrations

Grosset & Dunlap

ISBN 978-0-448-44713-1   10 9 8 7 6 5 4 3 2 1

No one was more excited for Easter than Angel Cake. Easter was her berry favorite holiday! She loved the holiday so much that on the day before Easter she invited her friends over to dye eggs and bake cookies.

"What should we do tomorrow?" asked Strawberry as she painted an egg pink.

"We could have an Easter picnic," suggested Orange Blossom.

Angel smiled to herself. She knew just how to make Easter extra-special for everyone!

On Easter morning, Strawberry Shortcake
went outside to take Custard and Pupcake for a
walk. But when she opened her front door, there
was a surprise waiting for her! It was a basket
with a note inside that read: *Follow the eggs for
an Easter surprise!*

"How berry exciting!" Strawberry exclaimed. It didn't take her long to spot the first egg. "There's one!"

"Where do you think the eggs will lead?" Custard asked.

"There's only one way to find out," Strawberry answered. "We'll have to follow the trail."

"I see another one!" Strawberry exclaimed as she walked with her pets down the Berry Trail.

There were beautifully painted
eggs hidden everywhere.

The trail of eggs led them to Apple Blossom Orchards.
There, Strawberry found Rainbow Sherbet and Blueberry
Muffin searching the tree branches.

"Hiya, Strawberry!" Blueberry exclaimed. "Are you on this Easter egg hunt, too?"

"I sure am," Strawberry answered. "Do you know where it leads?"

"Not yet," Rainbow answered.

"I guess we'll just have to keep looking," Strawberry said, giggling. "C'mon! I see another one."

The girls followed the trail of eggs to a field full of sweet-smelling roses.

Orange Blossom was already there searching for eggs.

"Did you get an Easter basket this morning, too?" Orange asked.

"We all did," Strawberry answered.

"I wonder who planned such a lovely surprise," said Orange.

"I'm not sure, but it looks like the trail goes to the River Fudge," Blueberry said as she gathered up another egg.

"Last one to the River Fudge is a rotten Easter egg!" Rainbow yelled.

When the girls reached the river, they found Ginger Snap and Huckleberry Pie gathering eggs.

"Looks like everyone is on the same hunt," said Huck when he saw the girls coming.

"Yup!" Strawberry answered. "But I think we're almost at the end. There's only one place left that we haven't been."

"Lead the way, Strawberry! I can't wait to see the surprise," said Rainbow.

"Something sure smells good!" Strawberry said as she led her friends down the Berry Trail.

When they walked into Cookie Corners, they saw a beautiful table decorated for Easter.

"Happy Easter!" Angel Cake exclaimed. She was holding a plate piled high with banana pancakes.
"Oh, Angel, what a wonderful surprise!" Strawberry said, hugging her friend.

"This is the best Easter ever!" Huck said happily.

"It's not over yet! I made a delicious brunch for everyone," Angel said as she led her friends over to the table. "Let's eat!"

Strawberry looked around the table at all of Angel Cake's treats and thought to herself, *nothing could be sweeter than spending Easter with my berry best friends.*